W9-BGW-088

Growing Readers

Otter Play

To my writing group: Barbara, Cathy, Kathryn, and Pat. Thanks for all your support and inspiration. And to Glenn, my paddling partner.
—N. L.

For Václav who lives rivers
—A. V.

Atheneum Books for Young Readers
An imprint of Simon & Schuster Children's Publishing Division
1230 Avenue of the Americas
New York, New York 10020

Book design by Angela Carlino
The text of this book is set in Janson.
The illustrations are rendered in watercolor.

First Edition
Printed in Hong Kong
10 9 8 7 6 5 4 3 2 1

Library of Congress Cataloging-in-Publication Data
Luenn, Nancy.
Otter play / by Nancy Luenn ; illustrated by Anna Vojtech.—1st ed.
p. cm.
Summary: A child watches otters at play and mirrors their behavior.
ISBN 0-689-81126-8
[1. Otters—Fiction. 2. Play—Fiction.] I. Vojtech, Anna, ill. II. Title.
PZ7.L9766Ot 1998
[E]—dc20
96-34026

Otter Play

written by
Nancy Luenn

illustrated by
Anna Vojtech

ATHENEUM
BOOKS FOR YOUNG READERS

Sunlight warms
the riverbank.
I stretch my arms
to touch
the cloudless sky.

In their burrow,
waking otters
yawn and stretch.
They nip
each other's
whiskers.

They slide
down cool,
damp earth
and *swish*—
they glide
into the river.

Our boat slides
off its trailer.
Mama rows
while Daddy
casts his line
to catch the flow.

Otter eyes
see people fishing,
drifting in the eddy.

My parents fish
but I watch otters
watching me.

Chittering,
the otters dive.

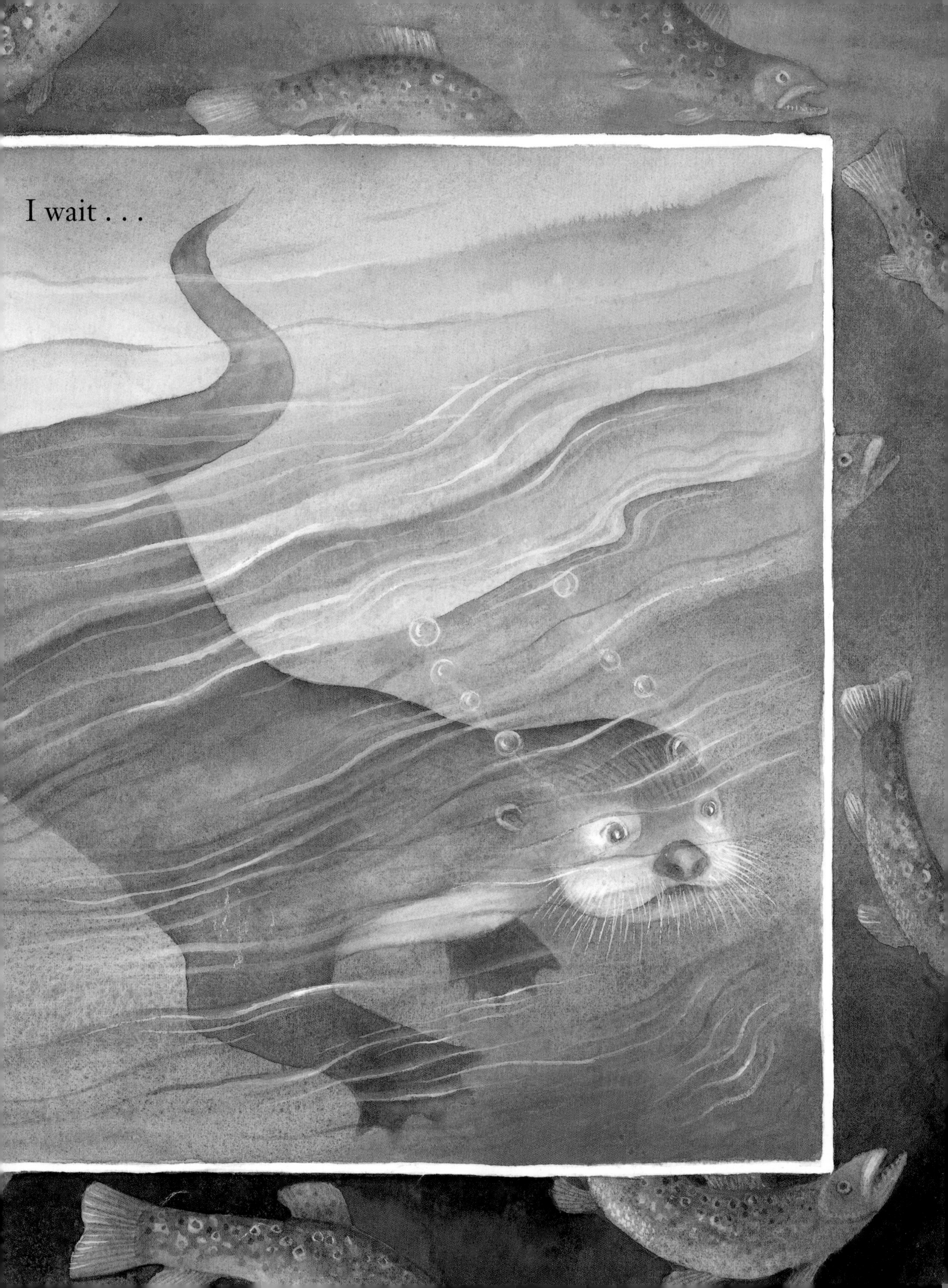

I wait . . .

the otters rise.

Their mouths
are full
of flapping trout.

Crunching bones,
the otters eat

while I munch
on an apple.

Bellies plump,
otters loll
upon a sunny log.

They wash
their fishy whiskers
clean.

I float
my apple boat
away . . .

a toy
for playful otters.

A clunk of oars;
the otters dive.
Our driftboat rides
the river waves.

Downstream
we set up camp.

Now otters ride
the leaping waves.
They frolic
in the eddy.

At our camp,
I frolic
like an otter
near the shore.

Otters tumble,
roll,
and wrestle
as the light
turns golden-gray.

Daddy and I
wrestle
on the cool
and scrunchy
sand.

Tired otters
scramble
up the slide
into their burrow.

“Bedtime!”
Mama calls.
I crawl inside
our bright, warm
tent.

Otters yawn
and curl together
in a dark,
warm ball.

I snuggle
in my sleeping bag
with memories
of the day.

They sleep
and dream
of frogs and fish.

I dream
of otter play.

More About Otters

River otters live in much of the United States and Canada. Once they were hunted and trapped until they disappeared from many places. More recently, the danger is due to changes people make in the natural environment. One of these changes is water pollution. When the water they live in is polluted, otters can't find enough food.

Now that some waters are cleaner, otters have returned to many of their former homes. They live in lakes, wetlands, and saltwater sounds, as well as on rivers. Otters often have two or three pups in the spring. The pups stay with their mother for almost a year. She teaches them to swim and hunt. Besides frogs and fish, otters eat crayfish, crabs, water insects, ducklings, and small mammals. They travel in pairs or in families, playing and exploring as they go.

NEW HANOVER COUNTY PUBLIC LIB.
3 4200 00491 1166